Tell Me Why

WHY?

It Gets Foggy

Nancy Robinson Masters

Published in the United States of America by Cherry Lake Publishing
Ann Arbor, Michigan
www.cherrylakepublishing.com

Content Adviser: Jack Williams, Fellow of the American Meteorological Society
Reading Adviser: Marla Conn, ReadAbility, Inc

Photo Credits: © Galyna Andrushko/Shutterstock Images, cover, 1, 19; © Olaf Naami/Shutterstock Images, cover,1, 5; © Anna Nahabed/Shutterstock Images, cover, 1, 7; © metriognome/Shutterstock Images, 9; © M. Pellinni/Shutterstock Images, 11; © Jaromir Chalabala/Shutterstock Images, 13; © FloridaStock/ Shutterstock Images, 15; © Michel Stevelmans/Shutterstock Images, 17; © Sergieiev/Shutterstock Images, 21

Library of Congress Cataloging-in-Publication Data

CIP data has been filed and is available at catalog.loc.gov.

Cherry Lake Publishing would like to acknowledge the work of the Partnership for 21st Century Skills. Please visit *www.p21.org* for more information.

Printed in the United States of America
Corporate Graphics

Table of Contents

A Bus Delay

"Are you going to eat your pancakes?" Mathis asked his sister, Tonya. She stood by the front door, watching for the school bus to arrive. Tonya could not see past the porch steps. Everything outside was covered with fog.

"I'm too excited to eat," Tonya answered. "Our class is going on a field trip to the zoo today."

Look closely at this photograph. Can you describe why it might be unsafe to drive a car or a bus in the fog?

Stripes painted on highways help drivers see the road when they are traveling in fog.

"Sorry, Tonya," Mathis said. "The weather reporter just said the school buses will be running late. The poor **visibility** makes the drivers go slowly. They can't see through the fog."

Tonya took a deep breath. "Does that mean we won't get to go on our field trip?"

Mathis tried to be cheerful. "Fog forms quickly and disappears quickly. Maybe the sun will burn off today's fog soon."

Fog can make you feel chilly on a cold day. It can also make you feel sweaty on a warm day.

The Fog Facts

Later that morning, the school bus finally arrived. Tonya's school day started almost three hours late. Her teacher, Mr. Hamilton, wanted to talk about the foggy morning. "Fog is a cloud sitting on the ground. The fog this morning formed when air near the ground turned colder than the air higher up," he said.

Tonya raised her hand. "But what is fog made of?" she asked.

"We see fog when the **water vapor**, a gas in the air, has reached its **dew point**. Each water droplet is smaller than a grain of sand," Mr. Hamilton explained.

Fog often occurs early in the morning.

Tonya's classmate Brandon raised his hand. "Are there different kinds of fog?" he asked.

Mr. Hamilton read aloud from a book about weather. "**Ground fog** forms mostly at night or before dawn. This is because at night, the ground cools more than the air does."

He continued, "A second kind of fog forms when warm air moves over a cooler surface. This happens most often when warm winds flow over cold oceans."

Fog is simply a cloud on the ground.

Staying Safe in Fog

Mr. Hamilton looked at the clock. "I know you're all excited about visiting the zoo," he said. "However, we will not be able to go today because of our late start."

Brandon asked, "Why aren't the buses delayed every time we have fog?"

Mr. Hamilton said that not all fog is thick enough to cause a delay. "Sometimes only mist is in the air. Water droplets in mist are not as close together as water droplets in fog. That's why mist is thinner than fog. You can see farther in mist than in fog."

Fog makes it hard to see traffic signals. It can even hide entire buildings.

Brandon said, "This morning my dad told me that people invented lighthouses because of fog."

"Good point," Mr. Hamilton said. "Lighthouses keep boats and ships safe in foggy weather. People built lighthouses near oceans, rivers, and lakes. The lighthouses use flashing lights and loud horns to guide ships through fog. Then ships sound their foghorns to warn other ships they're nearby."

Lighthouses sound horns and flash light signals to guide ships in foggy weather.

Tonya lived near the airport. She remembered seeing blinking lights on top of the tall tower. She raised her hand. "Do the lights on the towers help guide planes in fog?"

Mr. Hamilton smiled. "The green and white flashing lights you see at night at airports—called beacons—help pilots find runways. They are turned on during the day when fog or low clouds cover the airport."

How many foggy days are there each year where you live?

Airplane pilots receive fog warnings and other weather information before landing at airports with control towers.

Nature Needs Fog

Fog scientists study rainforests growing on mountains and in valleys. Some rainforests are called **fog forests**. Trees grow so thick in fog forests that rain cannot reach the soil. Fog carries **nutrients** down to the tree roots. In fog forests, many trees would not get enough water without the help from fog, even though it rains a lot in a rainforest!

Have you ever seen a 30-story building? That's how tall some giant redwood trees are in California. Branches from giant redwoods block rain from reaching the ground. Fog forms on the leaves and

Because these redwood trees are so tall and thick, their leaves catch the rain before it can reach the ground.

branches of these trees. The water that collects drips to the ground. This provides water to the tree roots, and the ferns and mosses growing under the trees.

Other living things also depend on fog. Some insects absorb fog to get the water they need. A frog doesn't swallow water at all. It absorbs water as fog through their skin.

Mathis knows there are many more things to learn about fog. Tonya hopes her class will visit the zoo when the sun is out!

Ask an adult to help you find out more about fog scientists. Look online or check for information in the library at your school.

Plants in this rainforest in Sri Lanka need fog to be able to grow. Sri Lanka is an island near the country of India.

Think About It!

Why does it take longer in winter for fog to burn off than in summer?

Go online to find a map showing the foggiest areas on earth. Are any of these areas close to where you live?

Make a list of the ways that fog forests and deserts are alike. Make another list of how they are different. Compare your lists. Where would you rather live?

People use huge nets called fog catchers to collect fog from the air. Look online for photos. What do you think people do with the fog water they catch?

Glossary

dew point (DOO POINT) the temperature when water vapor changes into water droplets

fog forests (FAWG FOR-ists) forests that depend on fog to survive

ground fog (GROUND FAWG) fog formed on the earth's surface from warm air rising into cold air

nutrients (NU-tree-uhntz) substances that living things need to grow and stay healthy

visibility (viz-uh-BIL-i-tee) the distance a person can see depending on light and weather

water vapor (WAW-tur VAY-pur) water in the form of gas

Find Out More

Books:

Ganeri, Anita. *Weather*. New York: Kingfisher Books, 2012.

Orr, Tamra B. *How Did They Build That? Lighthouse*. Ann Arbor, MI: Cherry Lake Publishing, 2012.

Web Sites:

National Park Service: Lighthouse History at Point Reyes
www.nps.gov/pore/historyculture/people_maritime_lighthouse.htm
Point Reyes in Northern California is the second-foggiest place in North America! Read about the history of its lighthouse.

Weather WizKids: Make Fog
www.weatherwizkids.com/experiments-fog.htm
Try this safe, easy experiment to learn how fog forms.

Index

About the Author

Nancy Robinson Masters and her husband, Bill, are airplane pilots. They live in the Elmdale community near Abilene, Texas. Nancy has written more than 40 books. She also travels around the world presenting programs in schools. To find out more about Nancy, visit her Web site at www.NancyRobinsonMasters.com.